Sultan's Triumphs
Five Tiny Tales

by Robin Epstein
Illustrated by the Disney Storybook Art Team

DISNEP PRESS
Los Angeles · New York

Editorial by Eric Geron
Design by Lindsay Broderick

For information address Disney Press, 1101 Flower Street, Glendale, California 91201.

Printed in China
First Hardcover Edition, September 2016
1 3 5 7 9 10 8 6 4 2
ISBN 978-1-4847-5245-6
FAC-025393-16183

For more Disney Press fun, visit www.disneybooks.com

Download the Whisker Haven Tales App

Welcome to Whisker Haven, dear!

I'm **Ms. Featherbon**, the hummingbird fairy and gatekeeper of Whisker Haven—and, from time to time, a party planner! I have so many wonderful places to show you . . . the **Pawlace**, **Whisker Haven Village**, **Whisker Woods**, **Whisker Sea**, and so much more. I manage this peaceful kingdom with help from all of the **Palace Pets**—Treasure, Petite, **Sultan**, Pumpkin, **Berry**, and Dreamy, to name a few. All those who reside in Whisker Haven cherish the **beauty of kindness**, the **glamour of helping others**, and, of course, the **royal heart of friendship**. . . .

Splendificent adventures await you in Whisker Haven!

Contents

Sultan Plays Fair
9

Sultan Spins
35

Sultan Gets Stuck
55

Sultan Lends a Paw
79

Sultan Soars
95

Sultan Plays Fair

"Today is going to be *rawr*-some!" exclaimed Sultan the tiger cub.

He soared on his magic carpet around his **Jungly Jungle Gym**, a sandy paradise with desert palm trees and a fun playhouse. Below him, **Pounce** the golden-colored kitten slid down the Jungly Jungle Gym's curvy slide.

"Woo-hoooo!" said Pounce.

"I can't wait to go to the Whisker Haven Carnival!" Sultan shouted.

"All the **Palace Pets** and **Critterzens** are going to have an amazing time!" said Pounce.

"But do you know what's going to be the most *amazingest* part of the day, Pounce?" asked Sultan.

"The most *amazingest*?" Pounce said. "Ooooh! I know!" he shouted. "Is there a fantastic feather display? I love feathers!"

Sultan shook his head.

"But what could be more amazing than fantastic feathers?" asked Pounce.

"Winning games!" Sultan yelled.

"Winning is the best part of any game!" said Sultan.

"Huh?" said Pounce, cocking his head.

"I hear there will be tons of games at the carnival!" said Sultan. "Well, I'm going to win every single one of them! I'm going to crush the competition!" Sultan roared and then laughed.

"Whoa! That's great! But how do you know you're going to win?" said Pounce.

"Because I'm rawr-some! That's how," said Sultan. He winked.

"You must practice all the time to become that rawr-some!" said Pounce.

Sultan laughed. "Practice?" he asked. "I don't need practice! I'm a talented tiger! The speediest, most bravest tiger in Whisker Haven!"

"But practice makes *purr*-fect," Pounce said.

"When you're this rawr-some, you're unbeatable!" said Sultan.

Just then, Ms. Featherbon, the hummingbird fairy and gatekeeper of Whisker Haven, flew overhead singing. "Palace Pets! Critterzens! Come to the meadow and join the fun! The Whisker Haven Carnival has now begun!"

As Ms. Featherbon flew away, she dropped one of her **tail feathers**. Pounce's eyes lit up at the sight of it. He scooped it up, shook it at Sultan, and said, "C'mon! Let's shake a tail feather!"

"Yeah! Let's rock and roar!" Sultan yelled. Then the tiger cub blasted off.

"Wait for me!" Pounce said, chasing him.

They moved as fast as their paws would carry them. When Sultan and Pounce arrived at the crowded meadow, they looked around at the **Whisker Haven Carnival** and grinned.

There were **rides** and **games** galore! Palace Pets and Critterzens started to line up. Sundrop, Whisker Haven's prettiest peacock, was putting up the last of the carnival decorations: **streamers**, **balloons**, and **lots of confetti**. While Sultan was looking around at all the carnival games, Pounce was staring at Sundrop, who stepped back to admire his work and shook out his tail feathers.

"Oooh, pretty feathers," said Pounce. "I really, really love feathers."

"Thanks!" said Sundrop.

Sundrop smiled and strutted past Pounce. But when he moved, **one of his tail feathers fell out!** Then he turned again, and two more feathers fell! He saw the three feathers on the ground. "Oh, me! Oh, my! Oh, no!" Sundrop cried.

Pounce walked toward him. Sundrop's eyes widened, his legs trembled, and **the proud peacock quickly backed away and ran out of the meadow**, away from the carnival.

While Pounce gathered Sundrop's feathers, **Sultan was on a mission: a mission to win**. And when Sultan strolled up to the first game booth, a device called the **Roar-O-Meter**, he knew his winning streak was about to begin.

"Whoever has the loudest roar wins," announced Mr. Chow the silver-blue cat.

Pumpkin the fluffy white puppy went first. "Okay! Here we go!" she said. "Rooo-arf!"

The Roar-O-Meter rose to 25 percent, and the crowd clapped their paws and hooves.

Nuzzles the shy little fox cautiously stepped up to the machine next and said, "Roar."

The Roar-O-Meter went to 2 percent.

Everyone looked at each other.

Nearby, a cricket chirped.

"Sorry. Loud noises actually startle me a bit," Nuzzles whispered.

"My turn!" Sultan exclaimed.

Nuzzles jumped and dashed away.

"Rooooaaaarrrr!" bellowed Sultan.

The Roar-O-Meter went to 100 percent. A bell rang, announcing him as the victor.

"That was amazing!" said Pounce.

"Thanks, pal!" said Sultan. "Now, what's next?" Sultan eyed the other games and saw the **Kibble Sack Race** was about to take place. "My tickling tiger tail!" said Sultan. "I'll win that race in no time!"

After jumping into his kibbles sack, Sultan hopped his way to yet another triumph!

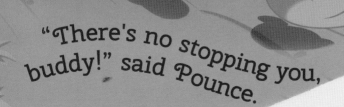

"There's no stopping you, buddy!" said Pounce.

"Thanks, Pounce!" Sultan said. "Now it's time to head into the 𝓗airy 𝓢cary 𝓕un 𝓗ouse!"

"You sure you want to do that, buddy?" Pounce asked, glancing at the fun house. "The Hairy Scary Fun House looks terribly . . . terrifying!"

"𝓣utu terrifying!" said Pumpkin.

"𝓦ell, 𝓘'm brave!" said Sultan. "𝓘'm not afraid!" He puffed out his chest and put on his bravest face before charging into the fun house.

Though Sultan was a little nervous going in, he explored every frightening nook and petrifying

cranny of that Hairy Scary Fun House. And by the time he came out the other end, he had a big smile on his face. "I'm the greatest tiger there ever was!" Sultan roared. "Watch my stripes! I'm unbeatable!" He turned to Pounce. "Now, what's the next carnival contest I'm going to win?"

Pounce turned to his left and pointed a paw. "Pony Shoe Toss!" he said.

"Great!" Sultan said, bounding over to the booth. Pounce followed. At the booth, Sultan found only one other pet waiting to compete against him.

Sweetie the blue sports-loving pony was practicing tossing pony shoes onto a shiny peg.

"Um . . . what do I have to do here, exactly?" Sultan whispered to Pounce.

"See that peg?" Pounce whispered. "You just have to toss the pony shoes around the peg."

"Just toss the shoes on the peg?" Sultan repeated, and Pounce nodded. "How easy is that?" Sultan took a pony shoe from Pounce, nodded at Sweetie, and smiled before letting the shoe soar!

It landed with a *THUD*, falling beyond the peg.

"*Rawr!* I didn't realize my own strength. . . ." Sultan said. "Pounce, another pony shoe, please?"

Pounce handed one to Sultan, and when Sultan threw it, this time it landed short of the peg.

"How rawr-ful!" Sultan exclaimed, grabbing the remaining pony shoes and tossing them, his aim getting worse with each throw. When Sultan was done, he looked at his toss-work. Not one pony shoe was remotely close to the peg!

"My turn!" Sweetie said, stepping beside Sultan. She tossed her first pony shoe.

CLANK!

The shoe landed right around the peg.

"Here we go again!" Sweetie shouted as she released another pony shoe.

CLANK!

Shoe number two hit the mark.

She threw shoes number three, four, and five.

CLANK! CLANK! CLANK!

The crowd of Palace Pets and Critterzens who had gathered around them went wild.

Ms. Featherbon swooped by the group. **"Congratulations, Sweetie!"** she sang out.

Everyone cheered.

But there was one pet who wasn't so happy about Sweetie's success. . . .

"Hey, that's not fair!" Sultan roared, stomping his paws and turning to face Sweetie.

"You only won Pony Shoe Toss because you're a pony!" Sultan told Sweetie.

"That could be true, Sultan," Sweetie replied. "But it's more likely that I won because I've been practicing day and night for this game. Tell me, how many hours did you spend training? Huh? Huh?"

"**How many hours?**" Sultan repeated. He scratched his head with his paw. "Well . . . zero."

"You didn't practice at all?" Sweetie asked. "But if you didn't practice, how did you expect to win?"

"**Because I'm me!**" Sultan said, smiling.

"You're not being a good sport," said Sweetie.

"Yeah, Sultan, I agree," said Pounce.

Sultan looked from face to face, and his smile slowly vanished. "What? What did I say?" he asked.

"It's like running," said Sweetie. "You're a fast runner, but the more you run, the faster you get!"

"Huh," said Sultan. "That makes sense."

"Since I practiced tossing pony shoes, it's no wonder I'm the ringer for the game!" Sweetie said.

"Sweetie, I owe you an a-*paw*-logy," said Sultan. "Practice really does make perfect. I'm sorry."

"A-*paw*-logy accepted!" said Sweetie.

"Sultan, what a splendificent sport you've proven to be!" said Ms. Featherbon.

"Thanks!" said Sultan. "Now, let's get back to the carnival games! I need as much practice as I can get before I challenge Sweetie to a rematch!"

"Oh, I can't wait!" Sweetie said with a smile.

Sultan Spins

"Attention, my dearies!" **Ms. Featherbon** sang as she swooped across the carnival grounds.

Palace Pets and **Critterzens** froze and looked up from the carnival games.

"What's going on?" Sultan asked.

"I'm not sure!" said Pounce.

"It's time to announce the next game of the carnival!" said Ms. Featherbon.

"And when it's happening!" added Teacup the brown puppy with floppy ears.

"That's right!" said Ms. Featherbon.

The crowd cheered.

"The Happy Hula-Hoop Hooplah will start at sunset!" said Ms. Featherbon.

"Ooh! I'd love to add Hula-Hoops to my collection!" said **Windflower** the blue raccoon. She gestured to her tepee filled with knickknacks.

"What are the rules?" asked Sweetie.

"*Who* knows?" said Fern the pink owl.

"I caaaaaaaaaaaaaaan't waaaaaaaaaaaaaaait," said **Miss Sophia** the sweet little sloth.

Taj the elephant peeked out from behind Windflower's tepee. "Can we play hide-and-seek instead?" he said, smiling.

"Hula-Hooping is fun!" said Tillie the orange-and-white cat with tutus on her head and waist.

"See you at sunset, my dears!" said Ms. Featherbon, zipping off through the blue sky.

But as the Palace Pets and Critterzens smiled and hollered, Sultan was slowly shaking his head.

"A Hula-Hoop contest?" he whispered to Pounce. "This isn't good."

"What's the problem, pal?" asked Pounce.

"I've never Hula-Hooped before!" said Sultan. "It's going to make winning this game really tough!"

"Oh!" Pounce said. "Well, that's not a problem!"

"It's not?" Sultan asked. "Why not?"

"Because you can practice!" said Pounce. "Practice makes *paw*-fect! Remember?"

Sultan's tail switched back and forth. "Oh, yeah! Like Sweetie did with the Pony Shoe Toss!" he said.

"Exactly!" said Pounce. "Follow me!"

Sultan trailed Pounce as he weaved among game booths, tents, and rides, until he stopped right in front of the fluffy white puppy, Pumpkin!

"Hi, Pounce. Hi, Sultan," she said.

"Hi!" Pounce said. "Can we ask you for a favor?"

"Yes! How can I help?" she asked.

"Could you please teach Sultan how to Hula-Hoop by sunset?" said Pounce.

"Of course I can!" said Pumpkin, twirling.

"*Rawr*-some!" said Sultan. "It'll only be a matter of time before I win! Let's practice at my Jungly Jungle Gym!" Sultan sped toward his jungle gym.

"Wait for meeeeeow!" Pounce shouted as he and Pumpkin raced to keep up.

Once they made it back to **Sultan's Jungly Jungle Gym**, Sultan's Hula-Hoop training began.

But when Sultan put the hoop around his hips, it dropped straight to the ground. "I don't get it. What am I doing wrong?" Sultan asked Pumpkin.

"You've got to roll your body," Pumpkin replied, demonstrating with a sparkly Hula-Hoop that spun around her waist. "Just imagine that you're dancing."

Sultan placed the hoop around his waist again and started to sway. **"It's working!"** he said, rolling. His Hula-Hoop moved with him perfectly.

"Stunning, Sultan!" said Pumpkin.

Pounce clapped. "Good job! If you keep practicing, you'll win the contest for sure!" he said.

"Pounce, that's exactly what I'm going to do for the rest of the afternoon till sunset!" said Sultan.

So Sultan practiced . . . and practiced . . . and practiced!

Soon Sultan was a Hula-Hoop master!

"Guys, look over there!" Pounce said.

Sultan and Pumpkin peered where he pointed.

"All I see is the sunset," said Pumpkin.

"*Purr*-cisely," said Pounce. "Don't you remember what Ms. Featherbon said?" He looked from Pumpkin to Sultan. "The Happy Hula-Hoop Hooplah starts at sunset!"

"That's *now*!" Sultan shouted. "Let's go!"

Quickly, they arrived back at the carnival.

Sultan lined up so he could participate in the

Happy Hula-Hoop Hooplah. While Sultan

waited, he saw who else would be competing.

Ahead of Sultan in line were Tillie, Taj, Teacup, Miss Sophia, Sweetie, Windflower, and Fern.

Ms. Featherbon landed beside them. "It's time for the Happy Hula-Hoop Hooplah!" she announced.

"Woo-hoo!" Sultan cheered.

"My, my, what is the rule again?" said Ms. Featherbon. "Ah, yes! Whoever keeps his or her Hula-Hoop moving the longest without letting it touch the ground wins! Now, pick up your hoops!"

As everyone picked up their Hula-Hoops, Sultan whispered to Pounce and Pumpkin, "It's going to be a ferocious competition, but I've been practicing!"

"Good luck, buddy!" said Pounce.

"Rawwwwrrr!" Sultan roared.

The competitors each held up their hoops.

"Woo-who!" said Fern. "We're ready!"

"Start your hooping!" said Ms. Featherbon.

Sultan spun his Hula-Hoop around his waist. "So far, so good!" he said as the hoop moved with his body. He glanced around at his competition.

Sultan's competitors were a sight to behold!

To Sultan's right, Teacup was twirling her Hula-Hoop around a teapot on her head! Sweetie was Hula-Hooping so fast it looked like she was in a tornado! And Tillie had fashioned her hoop to look like a tutu!

To Sultan's left, Fern was using two Hula-Hoops, twirling one around each wing. Soon Fern was in flight, rising into the clouds and out of sight!

Windflower had stacked all the remaining hoops around her body so that only her face could be seen peeking out the top. After a few seconds,

she started to **teeter**. Then she started to **topple**. Then she fell straight over and onto the ground! Taj, who could barely fit his Hula-Hoop around his belly, looked like he was wearing a tight belt. He tooted his trunk and slouched down. And Miss Sophia twirled her hoop **slowly** and **steadily**.

As Sultan continued to glance around at his friends, he couldn't help giggling. At the sound of his laughter, his friends looked at him and smiled, which only made Sultan laugh that much harder. **Soon he was rolling with laughter!**

Unfortunately, rolling with laughter made it very hard for Sultan to keep his Hula-Hoop in motion. **The jiggling of Sultan's giggling made his Hula-Hoop crash to the ground! But Sultan kept on laughing!**

Before long, everyone was laughing along! Hula-Hoop after Hula-Hoop dropped to the ground as Sultan's competitors' bellies shook with laughter. Pounce and Pumpkin laughed from the sidelines.

There was only one contestant still standing: Miss Sophia, who kept her Hula-Hoop spinning.

"My-ha-ha-ha!" said Ms. Featherbon. "Well, we have our winner. It's Miss Sophia! Well done, dear!"

Miss Sophia suddenly stopped twirling her hoop and looked around. "Meeeeeeeee?" she said.

"Congratulations!" everyone cheered.

"Thaaaaaaat's aaaaamaaaaaaziiiiiiing!" she said. A smile slowly spread across her face. But being the sensitive sloth that she was, she turned to Sultan. "Are youuuu ooookaaaay, Suuuuultaaaan? I knooooow hooooow muuuuuch youuuuu waaaaanted toooooo wiiiiiiiin thiiiiiiis conteeeeest."

"Winning is cool and all," said Sultan. "But I actually had a great time practicing with Pumpkin and Pounce. And then I had an even greater time Hula-Hooping with you all! Laughing and playing with my friends is the best prize I could ask for!"

"How simply marvelous!" said Ms. Featherbon. "Games aren't just about winning. They're about having fun!"

Everyone cheered.

And with that, they all went off to continue their carnival fun.

Sultan Gets Stuck

A giant pile of carnival prizes walked toward Sultan in the meadow under the evening stars.

Three colorful feathers poked out from the top of the heap of **balloons**, **glow necklaces**, **rubber duckies**, and **noisy gadgets**.

A few **Palace Pets** and **Critterzens** were so startled by the sight that they started backing away, hiding behind carnival rides and game booths.

But Sultan just smiled and walked right up to it. "**Pounce!**" said Sultan. "What's going on?"

"Whoooooaaaa!" Pounce yelped, losing his balance under the weight of all the prizes.

"Need some help?" Sultan asked.

"Please!" Pounce said.

Sultan unloaded the prizes from Pounce's arms. "Did you win all of these?" he asked.

"I sure did!" said Pounce. "At the Whisker Haven Carnival, everyone's a winner!"

"Rawr-some! Hey, where'd you win those?" Sultan asked, pointing to the colorful feathers at the front of Pounce's headdress.

"Oh, these?" Pounce replied, plucking one of the feathers from his headdress and holding it out. "I didn't win these feathers. I found them! Sundrop dropped them. Right over there!" Pounce pointed to the edge of the meadow. "C'mon! I'll show you!"

They raced to the edge of the meadow. There, they found another vibrant feather on the ground.

"Cooooooool!" Sultan shouted. "This feather is going to look great on me!" Sultan removed his hat and stuck the feather in his own headdress, just like Pounce had done.

"That's a fabulous feather, Sultan!" said Pounce.

"But you know what sticking a cool feather in your headdress makes you, right?" said Pounce.

"No, what's it make me, Pounce?" Sultan asked.

"It makes you a copycat!" said Pounce.

"A copy*cat*!" Sultan repeated with a laugh.

Sultan's laugh caused Pounce to laugh, too!

Suddenly, Pounce stopped laughing. His ears and tail pricked up and his whiskers began to twitch. **"What's going on, Pounce? What do you see? Smell? Hear?"** asked Sultan.

"Check it out!" Pounce replied, leading Sultan over to a trail of feathers he'd just spotted. **"Where do you think this trail leads?"**

"I have no idea," said Sultan. "But there's only one way to find out! Let's rock and roar!" he said.

Sultan and Pounce started following the trail.

Though usually Sultan and Pounce both liked to run, the trail was tricky, winding this way and that out of the meadow and into **Whisker Woods**. They moved slowly on the bending path, collecting more feathers.

Sultan and Pounce moved
deeper and deeper into the woods.

Pounce stopped in front of the woods' tallest trees. "Look at the tippity-top of that tree!" he said.

"Wow!" Sultan said, seeing the stunning feather resting up on the highest branch.

"I think that could be our most important feather yet," said Pounce.

Sultan nodded. "No doubt about it, Pounce. So what are you waiting for? Go and grab it!" he said.

"Right!" Pounce said. "Up, up, and away!" he yelled as he started climbing the tall tree.

Sultan was right behind him, scaling the bark.

They climbed . . .
and they climbed . . .
and they climbed.

It turned out the tree was much taller than either one of them had expected, and as they got higher, they had a great view over Whisker Haven, which was getting smaller beneath them. They could see **Whisker Haven Village**, the **Pawlace**, and **Whisker Sea** twinkling below.

"I think this is the tallest tree in Whisker Woods," Pounce said, gulping, as the two friends kept climbing higher and higher.

Finally, the beautiful peacock feather was only a paw's length away!

"Grab it!" Sultan hollered.

But when Pounce reached out his paw, the feather was still beyond his grasp. He pushed his arm out farther. Still nothing. He stretched his body, then tried to extend himself even more. No luck!

The feather was still too far away for Pounce to grab by himself.

"You know, Pounce, I'm happy to lend a paw if you need it," said Sultan. "If you need help, just say the word."

"If the word is please, then please!" said Pounce.

Sultan laughed. "Of course!" he said. "Just hop on my back and you should be able to reach it!"

Pounce scampered up Sultan's back and, sure enough, when he reached up, he snatched the feather right off the branch. "Got it!" he called.

"Rawr-some!" said Sultan. "That tickles my tiger's tail!"

Pounce admired his new feather, and he and Sultan made their way back down the tree.

"Thanks for helping me, Sultan. And if you ever need me to lend you a paw, just ask!" said Pounce.

Sultan laughed. "**Thanks, Pounce, but I never need help.** Remember, I'm a brave adventurer!" He puffed out his chest. "Now, let's rock and roar! We have more feathers to find!"

Racing back to the trail, the two friends spotted another bright and bold feather. It was stuck in a crack in a rock wall. As they roared in excitement, the feather fluttered down right in front of them!

"**Oh, yeah!**" Sultan shouted, grabbing it.

"We make a great team," Pounce said, smiling. "Hey, look! Is that another feather over on that log?"

The log was floating in Whisker Haven's bog.

"Sure is! And I'm gonna grab it!" said Sultan with a smile. "Catch this cat if you can!"

"Right behind you!" Pounce shouted.

Sultan felt like showing off a little, so when he got to the edge of the bog, he started dancing his way across the logs, skipping toward the feather.

"Be careful!" Pounce warned.

"Being careful is for scaredy-pets! I'm so brave, I could cross this log with my eyes closed," Sultan said, shutting his eyes and running.

Unfortunately for Sultan, the surface of the log wasn't quite even. So although he was brave, his bravery didn't stop him from tripping and losing his balance. "Rooooa-ah!" he yelled as he fell off the log and into the mucky bog.

"Sultan, are you okay?" Pounce said, racing over. "Take my paw." He extended his paw so Sultan could grab on and lift himself out of the bog.

"Thanks, but no thanks. I got this!" Sultan said as he tried hoisting himself up.

But getting unstuck from the bog was a lot harder than Sultan expected. He puffed up his chest, let out a roar, and with all his might he yanked and yanked his legs, trying to get them free.

But it was no use.

Sultan was stuck.

"Hey, Sultan, are you sure you don't need any help?" Pounce asked.

"I told you, Pounce, I'm fine!" Sultan replied. But even as he said it, he could feel himself starting to sink deeper into that murky bog. And the more he tried to paddle his way out, the deeper he seemed to go!

Sultan sighed. "Pounce?" he hesitantly murmured. "Could I . . . get a little help?"

"Finally!" said Pounce, reaching out his paw. "Now it's my turn to lend a paw to a friend in need."

Sultan took Pounce's paw, and Pounce pulled his friend up out of the muddy bog in a flash!

Once Sultan was back on the log, he shook all of the bog water out of his coat. Then he nodded at Pounce. "Thanks!" he said. "You saved me!"

"Of course!" Pounce said. "That's what friends are for!"

"It was so much easier to get out of that bog with your help," said Sultan. "I should have asked you for help as soon as I fell."

"You should have!" said Pounce with a smile.

Sultan's tail twitched. "Guess I thought I'd seem like a scaredy-cat," he said.

"Even the proudest, fiercest, bravest tigers ask for help sometimes," Pounce said with a laugh.

"Yeah, you're right," said Sultan, smiling. "**And I promise to ask for help if I ever need it again.** Not that I ever will!" He laughed. "Ha, ha . . . Sometimes it's hard for a tiger to change his stripes. But I'm learning! Now, let's rock and roar!"

The two friends raced off, leaving the bog far behind them.

Sultan Lends a Paw

"Hey, did you hear that?" Sultan asked Pounce, romping through **Whisker Woods**.

"Yeah!" Pounce said. "What do you think it is?"

Sultan's ears perked up and his tail twitched as he looked all around in the darkness of the woods.

Pounce's eyes darted left and right. When Sultan looked his way, Pounce smiled and laughed. "Ha, ha. I'm not afraid," he said.

Sultan gulped, then he laughed, too. "Ha, ha. Me neither . . ." he said.

The noise sounded again. It was like the rustling of leaves combined with the snapping of twigs . . . and a really loud sniffle!

"And what's that?" Pounce asked, pointing toward a looming shadow that was getting bigger with every step it took in their direction. **Then the shadow stopped and vanished back into the trees and bushes!**

"I don't know what that is, Pounce," said Sultan, his eyes widening, "but as the most fearless pet in all of Whisker Haven, I think it's my duty to . . . run!"

"Run?" asked Pounce.

"I mean . . . run to find out," said Sultan, who tried to keep from quivering. "Ha, ha."

"Okay, Sultan, go for it!" Pounce said. "And be careful," he added in a whisper.

Sultan tracked the direction of the sound and realized whatever was making the noise was hiding in a bush to their right. He crept closer and closer.

"Really? Who is that?" said a familiar voice.

"It's Pounce and Sultan," said Pounce. "Is that you, Sundrop?" Pounce peered into the bush.

"Stop, Pounce! Don't look at me!" cried Sundrop.

"What? Why not?" asked Pounce.

"Do you need help?" asked Sultan. "We're happy to lend a paw."

"No," Sundrop said. "I don't need help. I'm just . . . I'm just . . . Oh, I can't bring myself to say it!"

"What's wrong?" asked Sultan.

Sundrop stepped out from the bush.

"I'm . . . I'm bald!" Sundrop said. "I'm so embarrassed! I lost all my feathers. I look terrible!"

"You don't look terrible," said Sultan. "You just don't look like the Sundrop everyone knows!"

"What happened to your feathers?" said Pounce.

"You should know!" said Sundrop. "You seem to have gathered them all up!" He pointed to the pile of feathers that Sultan and Pounce had collected.

"What we mean is, why did all your feathers fall out?" Pounce asked.

"Did you want to get rid of them?" asked Sultan.

"I didn't want to get rid of them, Sultan. I molted," said Sundrop.

"But it's not even hot out today," Sultan said.

"Not melted," Pounce said. "Molted."

"What does *molted* mean?" asked Sultan.

"It means all my feathers fell out today," explained Sundrop, "which is why I look more like a bald eagle than a perfectly pretty peacock!"

Sundrop held back tears. "And even though molting is perfectly natural and happens to a lot of birds, it just makes me so embarrassed!" he cried.

"If it's perfectly natural, there's no reason to be embarrassed!" said Sultan.

"Thanks, but losing my feathers made me feel so flustered that I left the carnival and hid," said Sundrop. "I didn't want anyone to see me like this! And now here you are." He moved to hide again in the bush. "I don't want anyone else to see me until my feathers grow back."

"But that might take a while," said Sultan.

"Yeah! And we want you to come back to the carnival with us now to enjoy the rest of the night!" said Pounce. "Don't hide! C'mon! Let's go, Sundrop!"

"I really can't be seen," Sundrop said.

Sultan and Pounce exchanged glances.

"Sundrop, you look rawr-some with or without feathers," said Sultan.

"Yeah!" said Pounce. "Plus, everyone at the carnival is going to miss you!"

"If you come back to the carnival with us, we'll prove it!" said Sultan.

"The tiger talks truth," Pounce said.

"They'll miss me? What do you mean?" Sundrop asked, looking from Sultan to Pounce.

"Of course! While your feathers sure are fine, your friends love you for who you are, not for what you look like. You have the **royal heart of friendship**. You decorate Whisker Haven. And you always make everyone feel so warm and welcome!" said Sultan.

"Yeah!" said Pounce. "What he said!"

"Hmm," Sundrop said, nodding. "I hadn't thought about all that."

Sundrop sighed. "I think maybe you two are right. . . ." he said.

"We are!" Sultan and Pounce said together.

"It's nice to know that even though you guys appreciate my beautiful feathers, what you really like best about me is, well, *me*!" Sundrop said.

"Rawr-some!" Sultan roared. "Now that we're all in agreement, we have a carnival to get to!"

"We have more rides to ride and more games to play!" Pounce said.

"And we have friends to see!" Sundrop added.

The trio headed back through Whisker Woods and entered the meadow where the **Whisker Haven Carnival** was aglow with lights and music. Palace Pets and Critterzens laughed and whooped as they played games and rode rides.

Soon the friends were surrounded by Palace Pets and Critterzens.

"Where have you guys been?" asked Pumpkin.

"Yeah!" said Treasure. "We missed you guys!"

Ms. Featherbon swooped down beside them. "Hi, Sultan! Hi, Pounce! Hi, Sundrop!" she said. "There's something very different about you, Sundrop." She scratched her beak with her wing.

Sundrop blushed.

"You look different, yes, but in the most *splendificent* way!" said Ms. Featherbon, smiling.

"Yeah!" everyone cheered.

"And we're so happy to see you!" said Ms. Featherbon. "Now, let's keep this carnival going!"

And with that, Sultan, Pounce, and Sundrop joined all their friends in the carnival merriment.

"Thank you for lending a paw," Sundrop said to Sultan and Pounce.

"Any time," said Sultan. "We're just glad to see you smiling."

Sultan Soars

Sultan hopped back and forth, bouncing from paw to paw at the **Whisker Haven Carnival**.

It was nighttime in the meadow, and the carnival games and rides were in full swing. Sultan bounced alongside Pounce, **Berry**, and Sundrop. He jumped higher with each hop.

"**Sultan!**" Berry exclaimed as she watched her friend bouncing around. "**I know you're a tiger. But you're hopping so much, I'd say you were part bunny!**"

Sultan laughed. "Thanks, Berry! Maybe I'm actually your long-lost bunny cousin!" he said.

Pounce looked at Sultan's long tiger tail. "A bunny with a tail like that would be very interesting!" he said.

Sultan laughed and continued to bounce about, gaining more height.

"Since we know you're not a bunny, why are you bouncing so much, Sultan?" asked Sundrop.

Sultan pointed a paw to the night sky.

His friends glanced skyward, and they oohed.

There, shining brightly in front of them, was the carnival's giant **Ferris Hamster Wheel**!

"Since I was so busy playing games and collecting feathers earlier, I haven't been on that ride yet," Sultan said. "I want to make sure I ride the Ferris Hamster Wheel before the carnival closes."

"Now I understand!" Sundrop said.

"It looks like so much fun, I'm going to get in line with you!" said Berry.

"Me too!" said Pounce.

"Me three!" said Sundrop.

"**Are you guys sure?**" said Sultan. "The line is a little long. We may have to wait a while."

"Well, then it's a good thing I always carry snacks with me!" said Berry. With that, the bunny pulled out her emergency supply of blueberry muffins and started nibbling. "Anybody want one?"

Sultan, Pounce, Berry, and Sundrop stood in the long line of **Palace Pets** and **Critterzens**. After a while of bouncing and fidgeting, Sultan turned to his friends. "It's almost our turn!" he said. "I want to count how many there are ahead of us before it's our turn to ride," Sultan said. "Will you hold my place in line, Berry?"

"Certainly!" Berry said between muffin nibbles.

As Sultan sped toward the front, he passed by Dreamy, Petite, Treasure, and Pumpkin. Then he ran back to Pounce, Berry, and Sundrop.

"That's only four pets ahead of us," Sultan reported. "This is going to rock!"

"Did you count Brie?" Pounce asked, seeing the mouse running the wheel's controls.

"Oh! I didn't count her because she isn't going on the ride," said Sultan.

"Well, why not?" Sundrop asked.

"Because someone has to stay on the ground to make sure the wheel keeps spinning!" said Sultan, smiling. "Brie may be a mouse, but she sure does a great job at running this Ferris Hamster Wheel!"

"**Oh, yeah!**" Berry said. "I forgot about that!"

"Everyone in line! It's time!" Brie shouted, scampering off her chair at the controls. "Come one, come all, to the Ferris Hamster Wheel!"

"Purr-fect timing," Dreamy the kitten said. "Waiting makes me so tired, I was falling asleep...."

"Neeigh-ice!" Petite the yellow pony with pink mane exclaimed. "I've read all about Ferris Hamster Wheels before, and I can't believe I get to finally ride one!"

"Adventure ahoy!" said Treasure the orange-red kitten as she bounded up to her seat. "Me-wow, this is going to be fun!"

"It's going to be rawr-some!" Sultan said. He saw that Pumpkin, who was at the front of the line, wasn't moving into her seat. "What's the holdup, pup?" Sultan asked her.

"Oh," Pumpkin said, "well, I'm just kind of wondering how long we'll be on the ride. If I close my eyes tightly then open them after a few seconds, will the ride be over?" She studied the wheel.

Brie laughed. "Don't worry, Pumpkin," she said. "This ride lasts for a long, long time, so you'll have plenty of time to experience it."

"Oh," Pumpkin said. She started to tremble. "And how high up are you when you're at the top of the ride?"

Brie looked to the sky then whistled. "I don't quite know, but it's so high, you might have to duck your head so it doesn't hit the clouds!" she said.

"Yikes! That sounds like it could be too high!" Pumpkin yelled, hiding her eyes.

"I think Pumpkin is scared to go on the ride," Sultan whispered to his friends.

"Oh, my blueberry pie! I think you're right!" said Berry, nodding her head.

"As a brave tiger, I should show  her there's nothing to fear!" whispered Sultan. He turned to Pumpkin and said, "Watch me ride the wheel first, and then you can decide if you want to do it later, okay?"

"But what if something bad happens up there?" Pumpkin cried out.

"Nothing bad is going to happen," Sultan said. "It'll be okay."

Pumpkin gulped. "I don't know. . . ."

"You don't have to join us. But the ride will be much more fun if you're there with us!" said Sultan. "Totally up to you!"

Pumpkin looked at her friends. They all looked at her with smiles on their faces. She smiled and took Sultan's paw. "Okay," she said. "I'll join you."

"Are you sure?" asked Sultan. "It's up to you!"

"Yes," said Pumpkin. "It'll be tutu terrific!"

"Okay!" Brie said. "Palace Pets, please take your places in your seats and fasten your seatbelts!"

The pets climbed aboard the Ferris Hamster Wheel two by two, one pair at a time. Sundrop went with Pounce. Berry went with Treasure. Dreamy went with Petite. And last but not least, Sultan and Pumpkin climbed aboard the ride together. They settled into their cart and fastened their seatbelts.

"Ready?" Brie said, winding up the wheel.

"Spaghetti!" Berry exclaimed.

"Meow-what?" asked Treasure.

"I don't know!" replied Berry. "I just got so excited, I started getting hungry."

Sultan laughed. Then he noticed that Pumpkin had started shaking again.

She squeezed her eyes shut and held the bar in front of her.

Sultan glanced over at her. "Hey, you doing okay?" he asked.

Pumpkin nodded, keeping her eyes closed. "Oh, yes, thank you, Sultan. I'm just *paw*-ful," she replied. "I mean, *paw*-fect! Ha, ha!" When the wheel began to spin, Pumpkin yelped.

"Meowzers!" Treasure said, grinning and looking down at the carnival as the pets rose higher.

"This feels like a dream," Dreamy said as the wheel began to spin faster and all of the Palace Pets on board (except for Pumpkin, who had her eyes closed) got a full view of Whisker Haven.

"This isn't so bad," said Pumpkin.

Sultan and his friends soared in the sky, swinging gently in their carts.

"Woo!" shouted Sultan.

The wheel kept on spinning, making for a smooth and comfortable ride until . . .

CRRRREEEAAAAAK!

"What was that?" Pumpkin asked, bolting upright and snapping open her eyes.

"I'm sure it was noth—" Sultan started to say. But before he got to finish, the Ferris Hamster Wheel came to a grinding halt!

Pumpkin jumped up in her seat, causing their cart to swing wildly.

"What's happening?" Pumpkin shouted. "I was trying so hard to be brave, but I'm really, really, *really* afraid of heights. And this isn't helping! Ah! We're so very high up!"

"No need to fear!" Brie shouted up from the ground below. "Everything's going to be fine. Just a little ghost in the machine!"

"What?" Pumpkin screamed. "A ghost?"

"No, sorry! That's just an expression!" Brie said.

"Oh," said Pumpkin.

"I just mean there's a little bug in the system," said Brie. "I'll get it smoothed out in just a jiffy!"

Seeing how scared Pumpkin was, Sultan took her paw. "Here, Pumpkin, if you're feeling scared, just squeeze my paw!"

Pumpkin nodded then gave Sultan's paw a mighty squeeze.

"ROOOOAWWWRRR-*ouch*!" Sultan exclaimed as she squeezed his paw even harder. "I guess you are really, really, really scared."

"I'm tutu terrified!" Pumpkin cried.

"It's going to be okay, Pumpkin," said Sultan.

"I have an idea. . . ." Dreamy said, yawning. "But I'm too tired to . . . remember what it is. . . . Good night."

"Hey, Pumpkin," Petite shouted up from her cart. "One of the things that always amazes me about you is that when you get up on stage, you're not nervous at all. But when I'm on stage I get the willies. How do you do it? How do you keep calm?"

"I—I don't know," Pumpkin said, and then she closed her eyes again, imagining a stage beneath her feet and bright lights shining up at her.

Pumpkin let go of Sultan's paw. With the image of a stage in her mind, Pumpkin started dancing, moving her arms about. "It's time for a dance party!" she said. "Let's all dance!"

The Palace Pets looked at one another and all started moving their arms about like Pumpkin!

Pumpkin opened her eyes to see all of her friends grooving along with her. Much to her surprise, she discovered that while they'd been dancing, Brie had gotten the wheel turning again.

Pumpkin and Sultan's cart glided to the ground.

"Look!" said Sultan.
"You did it!"

Pumpkin hopped out of the cart and twirled onto the grass. "Phew!" she said. "I've never been happier to have my paws back on the ground! It feels tutu terrific!"

Sultan smiled at her. "You admitted your fear, you faced it, and you came out on top!" he said.

"I actually got *stuck* at the top," Pumpkin corrected him with a giggle.

"Well, I still think it was a pretty brave thing to do!" said Sultan.

"Me too!" said Petite.

"Me three. . . ." yawned Dreamy.

"Meeee-wow!" added Treasure.

"Yeah!" said Pounce.

"Nice work!" said Sundrop.

"Aw, thanks, guys!" Pumpkin said. "I'm so happy that my friends were here to help me through this."

Sultan gave his friend Pumpkin a big hug. He was impressed by her bravery and happy to have her and all the others as his good friends.

"Next time, you don't have to do something you don't want to do," said Sultan. "We'll still love you even if you don't go on high-flying rides with us!"

"Thanks, Sultan," said Pumpkin, smiling.

Ms. Featherbon flew into view and landed on the controls of the Ferris Hamster Wheel. "Well, my dears, the Whisker Haven Carnival is coming to a close. Did you all have a royally good time?" she asked.

"Yes!" they all hollered.

"We had a great time at the carnival!" Sultan cheered.

"Hearts! Hooves! Paws!" said his friends. They huddled and hugged as the lights in the Whisker Haven Carnival began to go out.

"Is it finally bedtime?" asked Dreamy.

Everyone laughed.

Good-bye for now!

Check out *Treasure's Adventures,* *Petite's Great Feats,* **and more!**

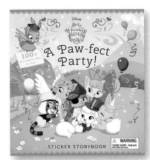

For more fun, download the Palace Pets in Whisker Haven App today!

disneypalacepets.com

Go-Kart Instructions

Step 1: Pop out all of the go-kart pieces.

Step 2: Insert the pieces into the go-kart bottom by matching the letters on the pieces with the letters on the go-kart bottom. *Roar*-some!

Step 3: Place Sultan inside of the go-kart and race off for adventure!